# THE GREEN MIST

*To Lindsey and Emily, sunbeams both!*

The text of this book is set in Bulmer.
The illustrations are watercolor, reproduced in full color.

This story is based on a tale of the same name from Lincolnshire England, likely dating
to the eighteenth-century. A version of "The Green Mist" appears in M. C. Balfour's
*Legends of the Lincolnshire Cars*, Folk-Lore, II, London, 1891.

In the old days it was believed that mysterious forces controlled the good and bad
happenings in people's lives. Within the soil (mools) and in the cracks of houses,
mysterious beings were thought to live. So it was that people practiced a series of rituals
throughout the year in an attempt to influence what they could not see and did not
understand.

*Library of Congress Cataloging-in-Publication Data*

The Green Mist / adapted and illustrated by Marcia Sewall.
p.   cm.
A version of "The Green Mist" appears in M. C. Balfour's *Legends of the
Lincolnshire Cars*, Folk-Lore, II, London, 1891.
Summary: A retelling of a Lincolnshire, England, tale, probably eighteenth-century,
in which a dying child is made well by the spring rituals intended to placate the
mischievous beings hiding in the earth.
ISBN 0-395-90013-1
[1. Folklore—England.]   I. Title.
PZ8.1.S4588Gr    1999
398.2'0942'02—dc21                          97-42615   CIP AC

Manufactured in the United States of America
BVG 10 9 8 7 6 5 4 3 2 1

# THE GREEN MIST

ADAPTED AND ILLUSTRATED BY

MARCIA SEWALL

HOUGHTON MIFFLIN COMPANY

BOSTON 1999

Have you ever watched the Green Mist rise from the mools at the coming of spring?

And have you heard of the bogles and all the horrid things that roamed the earth in the old times? In those days, if you listened hard, you could hear them in tiny squeaks and tappings. They hid in cracks and lived in cinders and slept within the fields. My grandfather said he'd heard tell how folks once worried terribly about them and behaved so as to keep them friendly.

In the early days there were, so to say, two churches: the
one with priests and such, the other just a lot of old ways kept
all hidden-like amidst the people.

So it was at darkling every night they'd bear lights in their hands and walk round their houses saying words such as they could scarcely understand themselves, wishing to keep the mischancy beings away.

On autumn evenings they sang hush-a-bye songs in the
fields, for the earth was tired and sinking to sleep. They
feared the long dark winters, for, as the earth slept, the bogles
had nothing to do but make mischief.

At Christmastime there were grand church services to
celebrate the birth of the Christ child, but in the cottages
there were yule cakes and candles and secret doings to bring
in the New Year.

Early spring was a time when people particularly went in
for spells and prayers and such. To each field in town they'd go
and lift a spade of earth from the mools, murmuring the old
words, hoping to befriend the mischievous beings hiding there.

They thought a great deal about the sun, for they reckoned
it had made the earth and brought good and ill luck to all
people living upon it.

And never knowing the strangeness of it all, they waited
and watched for the Green Mist to awaken the sleeping land.

Now, there was one family who sang the hush-a-bye songs every autumn and waked the earth from its sleeping each spring just as their grandfathers had done. But all the same, sickness and whatnot had been bad in the place that year.

When the ox plowed the field in figure eights, they knew there was trouble about.

Then the well went dry.

Soon the cow gave no milk.

That winter brought the worst of all! Through the cold dark days the daughter, once a romping lass, sat all white and shaking by the fire. Yet when the sun shone, she danced like a will-o'-the-wisp and stretched her arms as if she lived only in the brightness of the sun.

One day the little girl could not stand on her feet any more than a newborn baby and lay at the window watching winter slowly creep away.

"Oh, Mother!" she kept saying. "If only I could wake the spring with you again, maybe the Green Mist would make me well like the trees and flowers and corn soon to come."

Her mother comforted her and promised that she would take her daughter to the fields at the waking of spring, promised that she would grow as strong and straight as ever.

But day after day the girl waned like a fading snowflake.

Finally it was time for spring to return. Every morning as
the sun began to rise, folks stood ready with an offering of salt
and bread, watching and waiting for the Green Mist to tell

them that the earth was awake, that seeds would burst forth,
and life would come to all growing things.

Alas, the girl was naught but a bag-o'-bones, too weak to be taken to the fields with the rest, so her mother promised instead to carry her to the doorsill.

"If the Green Mist don't come in the dawning morning, I'll not be able to wait for it any longer. The mools is calling, Ma, and seeds is bursting that will bloom over my head. I shall not live. I know it well."

"Shhh! Shhh!" The mother hushed her child in fear, for the bogles were listening!

But dawn of the next day brought the Green Mist. It came
from the mools and wrapped itself around everything.

It was green as grass in summer sunshine and sweet
smelling as the herbs of spring.

Once carried to the doorsill, the child crumbled the bread and salt onto the earth with her own thin hands and said the strange old words of welcoming to the new spring.

Her mother then took her back to bed by the window, where she slept like a baby and dreamed of summer and flowers and happiness.

Whether it was the Green Mist that did it, I can't tell you more than my grandfather said, but from that day the little lass grew stronger and prettier than ever.

By the time the cowslips budded she was laughing and running about like a sunbeam. Once again she was the joyful maiden who danced like a bird on sunlit grass by the garden's nodding blossoms and yellow blooms.

Seeds planted that spring sprouted from the mools and grew in plenty. Day after day a touch of mist followed the bright sunshine of morning.

Across the land the softly colored fields were again dotted
with haycocks.

And every night folks walked round their cottages
murmuring the old words, their candles twinkling in the
darkness.